THE CAIRN ON THE HEADLAND

BY

ROBERT E. HOWARD

British Library Cataloguing-in-Publication Data
A catalogue record for this book is available from the
British Library

Robert E. Howard

Robert Ervin Howard was born in Peaster, Texas in 1906. During his youth, his family moved between a variety of Texan boomtowns, and Howard – a bookish and somewhat introverted child – was steeped in the violent myths and legends of the Old South. Although he loved reading and learning, Howard developed a distinctly Texan, hardboiled outlook on the world. He became a passionate fan of boxing, taking it up at an amateur level, and from the age of nine began to write adventure tales of semi-historical bloodshed. In 1919, when Howard was thirteen, his family moved to the Central Texas hamlet of Cross Plains, where he would stay for the rest of his life.

At fifteen Howard began to read the pulp magazines of the day, and to write more seriously. The December 1922 issue of his high school newspaper featured two of his stories, 'Golden Hope Christmas' and 'West is West'. In 1924 he sold his first piece – a short caveman tale titled 'Spear and Fang' – for $16 to the not-yet-famous *Weird Tales* magazine. He published with the magazine regularly over the next few years. 1929 was a breakout year for Howard, in that the 23-year-old writer began to sell to other magazines, such as *Ghost Stories* and *Argosy*, both of whom had previously sent him hundreds of rejection slips. In 1930, he began a correspondence with weird fiction master H. P. Lovecraft which ran up to his death six years later, and is regarded as one of the great correspondence cycles in all of fantasy literature.

It was partly due to Lovecraft's encouragement that Howard created his most famous character, Conan the Cimmerian. Conan – a barbarian-turned-King during the Hyborian Age, a mythical period of some 12,000 years ago – featured in seventeen *Weird Tales* stories between 1933 and 1936, and is now regarded as having spawned the 'sword and sorcery' genre, making Howard's influence on fantasy literature comparable to that of J. R. R. Tolkien's. The Conan stories have since been adapted many times, most famously in the series of films starring Arnold Schwarzenegger.

Howard was enjoying an all-time high in sales by the beginning of 1936, but he was also deeply upset by the ill health of his mother, who had fallen into a coma. On the morning of June 11, 1936, he asked an attending nurse whether she would ever recover, and the nurse replied negatively. Howard walked to his car, parked outside the family home in Cross Plains, and shot himself. He died eight hours later, aged just thirty.

THE CAIRN ON THE HEADLAND

And the next instant this great red loon was shaking me like a dog shaking a rat. "Where is Meve MacDonnal?" he was screaming. By the saints, it's a grisly thing to hear a madman in a lonely place at midnight screaming the name of a woman dead three hundred years.

--The Longshoreman's Tale.

"This is the cairn you seek," I said, laying my hand gingerly on one of the rough stones which composed the strangely symmetrical heap.

An avid interest burned in Ortali's dark eyes. His gaze swept the landscape and came back to rest on the great pile of massive weather-worn boulders.

"What a wild, weird, desolate place!" he said. "Who would have thought to find such a spot in this vicinity? Except for the smoke rising yonder, one would scarcely dream that bey and that headland lies a great city! Here there is scarcely even a fisherman's but within sight."

"The people shun the cairn as they have shunned it for centuries," I replied.

"Why?"

"You've asked me that before," I replied impatiently. "I can only answer that they now avoid by habit what their ancestors avoided through knowledge."

"Knowledge!" he laughed derisively. "Superstition!"

I looked at him sombrely with unveiled hate. Two men could scarcely have been of more opposite types. He was slender, self-possessed, unmistakably Latin with his dark eyes and sophisticated air. I am massive, clumsy and bearlike, with cold blue eyes and tousled red hair. We were countrymen in that we were born in the same land; but the homelands of our ancestors were as far apar as South from North.

"Nordic superstition," he repeated. "It cannot imagine a Latin people allowing such a mystery as this to go unexplored all these years. The Latins are too practical too prosaic, if you will. Are you sure of the date of this pile?"

"I find no mention of it in any manuscript prior to 1014 A.D.," I growled, "and I've read all such manuscripts extant, in the original. MacLiag, King Brian Boru's poet, speaks of the rearing of the cairn immediately after the battle, and there can be little doubt that this is the pile referred to. It is mentioned briefly in the later chronicles of the Four Masters, also in the Book of Leinster, compiled in the late 1150's, and again in the Book of Lecan, compiled by the MacFirbis about 1416. All connect it with the battle of Clontarf, without mentioning why it was built."

"Well, what is the mystery about it?" he queried. "What more 'natural than that the defeated Norsemen should rear a cairn above the body of some great chief who had fallen in the battle?"

"In the first place," I answered, "there is a mystery concerning the existence of it. The building of cairns above the dead was a Norse, not an Irish, custom. Yet according to the chroniclers, it was not Norsemen who reared this heap. How could then have built-it immediately after the battle, in which they had been cut to pieces and driven in headlong flight through the gates of Dublin? Their chieftains lay where they had fallen and the ravens picked their bones. It was Irish hands that heaped these stones."

"Well, was that so strange?" persisted Ortali. "In old times the Irish heaped up stones before they went into battle, each man putting a stone in place; after the battle the living removed their stones, leaving in that manner a simple tally of the slain for any who wished to count the remaining stones."

I shook my head.

"That was in more ancient times; not in the battle of Clontarf. In the first place, there were more than twenty thousand warriors, and four thousand fell here; this cairn is not large enough to have served as a tally of the men killed in battle. And it is too symmetrically built. Hardly a stone has fallen away in all these centuries. No, it was reared to cover something."

"Nordic superstitions!" the man sneered again.

"Aye, superstitions if you will!" Fired by his scorn, I exclaimed so savagely that he involuntarily stepped back; his hand slipping inside his coat. "We of North Europe had gods and demons before which the pallid mythologies of the South fade to childishness. At a time when your ancestors were lolling on silken cushions among the crumbling marble pillars of a decaying civilization, my ancestors were building their own civilization in hardships and gigantic battles against foes human and inhuman.

"Here on this very plain the Dark Ages came to an end and the light of a new era dawned on the world of hate and anarchy. Here, as even you know, in the year 1014, Brian Boru and his Dalcassian ax wielders broke the power of the heathen Norsemen forever--those grim anarchistic plunderers who had held back the progress of civilization for centuries."

"It was more than a struggle between Gael and Dane for the crown of Ireland. It--was a war between the White Christ and Odin, between Christian and pagan.. It was the last stand of the heathen--of the people of the old, grim ways. For three hundred years the world had writhed beneath the heel of the Viking, and here on Clontarf that scourge was lifted forever.

"Then, as now, the importance of that battle was underestimated by polite Latin and Latinized writers and historians. The polished sophisticates of the civilized cities of the South were not interested in the battles of barbarians in the remote northwestern corner of the world--a place and peoples of whose very names they were only vaguely aware. They only knew that suddenly the terrible raids of the sea kings ceased to sweep along their coasts, and in another century the wild age of plunder and slaughter had almost been forgotten-all because a rude, half-civilized people who scantily covered their nakedness with wolf hides rose up against the conquerors."

"Here was Ragnarok, the fall of the Gods! Here in very truth Odin fell, for his religion was given its death blow. He was last of all the heathen gods to stand before Christianity, and it looked for a time as if his children might prevail and plunge the world back into darkness and savagery. Before Clontarf, legends say, he often appeared on earth to his worshippers, dimly seen in the smoke of the sacrifices naked human victims died screaming, or riding the wind-torn clouds, his wild locks flying in the gale, or, appareled like a Norse warrior, dealing thunderous blows in the forefront of nameless battles. But after Clontarf he was seen no more; his worshippers called on him in vain with wild chants and grim sacrifices. They lost faith in him, who had failed them in their wildest hour; his altars crumbled, his priests turned

7

grey and died, and men turned--to his conqueror, the White Christ. The reign of blood and iron was forgotten; the age of the red-handed sea kings passed. The rising sun, slowly, dimly, lighted the night of the Dark Ages, and men forgot Odin, who came no more on earth."

"Aye, laugh if you will! But who knows what shapes of horror have-had birth in the darkness, the cold gloom; and the whistling black gulfs of the North? In the southern lands the sun shines and flowers bloom; under the soft skies men laugh at demons. But in the North, who can say what elemental spirits of evil dwell in the fierce storms and the darkness? Well may it be that from such fiends of the night men evolved the worship of the grim ones, Odin and Thor, and their terrible kin."

Ortali was silent for an instant, as if taken aback by my vehemence; then he laughed. "Well said, my northern philosopher! We will, argue these questions another time. I could hardly expect a descendant of Nordic barbarians to escape some trace of the dreams and mysticism of his race. But you cannot expect me to be moved.. by your imaginings, either. I still believe that this cairn covers no grimmer secret than a Norse chief who fell in the battle-and really your ravings concerning Nordic devils have no bearing on the matter. Will you help me tear into this cairn?"

"No," I answered shortly.

"A few hours' work will suffice to lay bare whatever it may hide," he continued as if he had not heard. "By the way, speaking of superstitions, is there not some wild tale concerning holly connected with this heap?"

"An old legend says that all trees bearing holly were cut down for a league in all directions, for some mysterious reason," I answered sullenly. "That's another mystery. Holly was an important part of Norse magic-making. The Four Masters tell of a Norseman-a white bearded ancient of wild aspect, and apparently a priest of Odin-who was slain by the natives while attempting to lay a branch of holly on the cairn, a year after the battle."

"Well," he laughed, "I have procured a sprig of holly- -see?--and shall wear it in my lapel; perhaps it will protect me against your Nordic devils. I feel more certain than ever that the cairn covers a sea king-and they were always laid to rest with all their riches; golden cups and jewel-set sword hilts and silver corselets. I feel that this cairn holds wealth, wealth over which clumsy-footed Irish peasants have been stumbling for centuries, living in want and dying in hunger. Bah! We shall return here at midnight, when we may be fairly certain that we will not be interrupted--and you will aid me at the excavations."

The last sentence was rapped out in a tone that sent a red surge of blood-lust through my brain. Ortali turned and began examining the cairn as he spoke, and almost involuntarily my hand reached out stealthily and closed on a wicked bit of jagged stone that had become detached from one of the boulders. In that instant I was a potential murderer if ever one walked the earth. One blow, quick, silent and savage, and I would be free forever from a slavery bitter as my Celtic ancestors knew beneath the heels of the Vikings.

As if sensing my thoughts, Ortali wheeled to face me.. I quickly slipped the stone into my pocket, not knowing whether he noted the action. But he must have seen the red killing instinct burning in my eyes, for again he recoiled and again his hand sought the hidden revolver.

But he only said: "I've changed my mind. We will not uncover the cairn tonight. Tomorrow night, perhaps. We may be spied upon. Just now I am going back to the hotel."

I made no-reply, but turned my back upon him and stalked moodily away in the direction of the shore. He started up the slope of the headland beyond which lay the city, and when I turned to look at him, he was just crossing the ridge, etched, clearly against the hazy sky. If hate could kill, he would have dropped dead. I saw him in a red-tinged haze, and the pulses in my temples throbbed like hammers.

I turned back toward the shore, and stopped suddenly. Engrossed with my own dark thoughts, I had approached within a few feet of a woman before seeing her. She was tall and strongly made, with a strong stern face, deeply lined and weather-worn as the hills. She was dressed in a manner strange to me, but I thought little of it, knowing the curious styles of clothing worn by certain backward types of our people.

"What would you be doing at the cairn?" she asked in a deep, powerful voice. I looked at her in surprise; she spoke in Gaelic, which was not strange of itself, but the Gaelic she used I had supposed was extinct as a spoken language: it was the Gaelic of scholars, pure, and with a distinctly archaic flavour. A woman from some secluded hill country, I thought, where the people still spoke the unadulterated tongue of their ancestors.

"We were speculating on its mystery," I answered in the same tongue, hesitantly, however, for though skilled in the more modern form taught in the schools, to match her use of the language was a strain on my knowledge of it. She shook her head slowly." I like not the dark mart who was with you," she said somberly. "Who are you?"

"I'm an American, though born and raised here," I answered. "My name is James O'Brien."

A strange light gleamed in her cold eyes.

"O'Brien--You are of my clan. I was born an O'Brien. I married a man of the MacDonnals, but my heart was ever with the folk of my blood."

"You live hereabouts?" I queried, my mind on her unusual accent.

"Aye, I lived here upon a time," she answered, "but I have been far away for a long time. All is changed-changed. I would not have returned, but I was drawn back by a call you would not understand. Tell me, would you open the cairn?"

I started and gazed at her closely, deciding that she had somehow overheard our conversation.

"It is not mine to say," I answered bitterly. "Ortali my companion--he will doubtless open it and I am constrained to aid him. Of my own will I would not molest it."

Her cold eyes bored into my soul.

"Fools rush blind to their doom," she said sombrely. "What does this man know of the mysteries of this ancient land? Deeds have been done here whereof the world re-echoed. Yonder, in the long ago, when Tomar's Wood rose dark and rustling against the plain of Clontarf, and the Danish walls of Dublin loomed south of the river Liffey, the ravens fed on the slain and the setting sun lighted lakes of crimson. There King Brian, your ancestor and mine, broke the spears of the North. From all lands they came, and from the isles of the sea; they came in gleaming mail and their horned helmets cast long shadows across the land. Their dragon-prows thronged the waves and the sound of their oars was as the beat of a storm.

"On yonder plain the heroes fell like ripe wheat before the reaper. There fell Jarl Sigurd of the Orkneys, and Brodir of Man, last of the sea kings, and all their chiefs. There fell, too, Prince Murrough and his son, Turlogh, and many chieftains of the Gael, and King Brian Boru himself, Erin's mightiest monarch."

"True!" My imagination was always fired by the epic tales of the land of my birth. "Blood of mine was spilled here, and, though I have passed the best part of my life in a far land, there are ties of blood to bind my soul to this shore."

She nodded slowly, and from beneath her robes drew forth something that sparkled dully in the setting sun.

"Take this," she said. "As a token of blood tie, I give it to you. I feel the weird of strange and monstrous happenings but this will keep you safe from evil and the people of the night. Beyond reckoning of man, it is holy."

I took it, wonderingly. It was a crucifix of curiously, worked gold, set with tiny jewels. The workmanship was extremely archaic and unmistakably Celtic. And vaguely within me stirred a memory of a long-lost relic described by forgotten monks in dim manuscripts.

"Great heavens!" I exclaimed. "This is--this must be--this can be nothing less than the lost crucifix of Saint Brandon the Blessed!"

"Aye." She inclined her grim head. "Saint Brandon's cross, fashioned by the hands of the holy man in long ago, before the Norse barbarians made Erin a red hell--in the days when a golden peace and holiness ruled the land."

"But, woman!" I exclaimed wildly. "I cannot accept this as a gift from you! You cannot know its value! Its intrinsic worth alone is equal to a fortune; as a relic it is priceless--"

"Enough!" Her deep voice struck me suddenly silent. "Have done with such talk, which is sacrilege. The cross of Saint Brandon is beyond price. It was never stained with gold; only as a free gift has it ever changed hands. I give it to you to shield you against the powers of evil. Say no more."

"But it has been lost for three hundred years!" I exclaimed. "How--I--here . . ."

"A holy man gave a it to me long ago," she answered. "I hid it in my bosom--long it lay in my bosom. But now I give it to you; I have come from a far country to give it to you, for there are monstrous happenings in the wind, and it is sword and shield against the people of the night. An ancient evil stirs in its prison, which blind hands of folly may break open; but stronger than any evil is the cross of Saint Brandon, which has gathered power and strength through the long, long ages since that forgotten evil fell to the earth."

"But who are you?" I exclaimed.

"I am Meve MacDonnal," she answered.

Then, turning without a word, she strode away in the deepening twilight while I stood bewildered and watched her cross the headland and pass from sight, turning inland as she topped the ridge. Then I, too, shaking myself like a man waking from a dream, went slowly up the slope and across the headland. When I crossed the ridge it was as if I had passed out of one world into another: behind me lay the wilderness and desolation of a weird medieval age; before me pulsed the lights and the roar of modern Dublin. Only one archaic touch was lent to the scene before me: some distance inland loomed the straggling and broken lines of an ancient graveyard, long deserted and grown up in weeds, barely discernible in the dusk. As I looked I saw a tall figure moving ghostily among the crumbling tombs, and I shook my head bewilderedly. Surely Meve MacDonnal was touched with madness, living in the past, like one seeking to stir to flame the ashes of dead yesterday. I set out toward where, in the near distance, began the straggling window--gleams that grew into the swarming ocean of lights that was Dublin.

Back at the suburban hotel where Ortali and I had our rooms, I did not speak to him of the cross the woman had given me. In that, at least, he should not share: I intended keeping it until she requested its return, which I felt sure she would do. Now as I recalled her appearance, the strangeness of her costume returned to me, with one item which had impressed itself on my subconscious mind at the time, but which I had not consciously realized. Meve MacDonnal had been wearing sandals of a type not worn in Ireland for centuries. Well, it was perhaps natural that with her retrospective nature she should imitate the apparel of the past ages which seemed to claim all her thoughts.

I turned the cross reverently in my hands. There was no doubt that it was the very cross for which antiquarians had searched so long in vain, and at last in despair had denied the existence of. The priestly scholar, Michael O'Rourke, in a treatise written about 1690, described the relic at length, chronicled its history exhaustively, and maintained that it was last heard of in the possession of Bishop Liam O'Brien, who, dying in 1955, gave it into the keeping of a kinswoman; but who this woman was, it was never known, and O'Rourke maintained that she kept her possession of the cross a secret, and that it was laid away with her in her tomb.

At another time my elation at discovering the relic would have been extreme, but, at the time, my mind was too filled with hate and smouldering fury. Replacing the cross in my pocket, I fell moodily to reviewing my connections with Ortali, connections which puzzled my friends, but which were simple enough.

Some years before I had been connected with a certain large university in a humble way. One of the professors with whom I worked-a man named Reynolds-was of intolerably overbearing disposition toward those whom he considered his inferiors. I was a poverty-ridden student striving for life in a system which makes the very existence of a scholar precarious. I bore Professor Reynolds' abuse as load as I could, but one day we clashed.

The reason does not matter; it was trivial enough in itself. Because I dared reply to his insults, Reynolds struck me and I knocked him senseless.

That very day he caused my dismissal from the university. Facing not only an abrupt termination of my work and studies, but actual starvation, I was reduced to desperation, and I went to Reynolds' study late that night intending to thrash him within an inch of his life. I found him alone in his study, but the moment I entered, he sprang up and rushed at me like a wild beast, with a dagger he used for a paperweight. I did not strike him; I did not even touch him. As I stepped aside to avoid his rush; a small rug slipped beneath his charging feet: He fell headlong, and, to my horror, in his fall the dagger in his hand was driven into his heart. He died instantly. I was at once aware of my position, I was known to have quarreled; and even exchanged blows with the man. I had every reason to hate him. If I were found in the study with the dead man, no jury in the world would believe that I had not murdered him. I hurriedly left by the way I had come, thinking that I had been unobserved. But Ortali, the dead man's secretary, had seen me. Returning from a dance, he had observed me entering the premises, and, following me, had seen the whole affair through the window. But this I did not know until later.

The body was found by the professor's housekeeper, and naturally there was a great stir. Suspicion pointed to me, but lack of evidence kept me from being indicted, and this same lack of evidence brought about a verdict of suicide. All this time Ortali had kept quiet. Now he came to me and disclosed what he knew. He knew, of course, that I had not killed Reynolds, but he could prove that I was in the study when the professor met his death, and I knew Ortali was capable of carrying out his threat of swearing that he had seen me murder Reynolds in cold blood. And thus began a systematic blackmail.

I venture to say that a stranger blackmail was never levied. I had no money then; Ortali was gambling on my future, for he was assured of my abilities. He advanced me money, and, by clever wire-pulling, got me an appointment in a large college. Then he sat back to reap the benefits of his scheming, and he reaped full fold of the seed he sowed. In my line I became eminently successful. I soon commanded an enormous salary in my regular work, and I received rich prizes and awards for researches of various difficult natures, and of these Ortali took the lion's share--in money at least. I seemed to have the Midas touch. Yet of the wine of my success I tasted only the dregs.

I scarcely had a cent to my name. The money that had flowed through my hands had gone to enrich my slaver, unknown to the world. A man of remarkable gifts, he, could have gone to the heights in any line, but for a queer streak in him, which, coupled with an inordinately avaricious nature, made him a parasite, a blood-sucking leech.

This trip to Dublin had been in the nature of a vacation for me. I was worn out with study and labor. But he had somehow heard of Grimmin's Cairn, as it was called, and, like a vulture that scents dead flesh, he conceived himself on the track of hidden gold. A golden wine cup would have been, to him, sufficient reward for the labour of tearing into the pile, and reason enough for desecrating or even destroying the ancient landmark. He was a swine whose only god was gold.

Well, I thought grimly, as I disrobed the bed, all things end, both good and bad. Such a life as I had lived was unbearable. Ortali had dangled the gallows before my eyes until it had lost its terrors. I had staggered beneath the load I carried because of my love for my work. But all human endurance has its limits. My hands turned to iron as I thought of Ortali, working beside me at midnight at the lonely cairn. One stroke, with such a stone as I had caught up that day, and my agony would be ended. That life and hopes and career and ambition would be ended as well, could not be helped. Ah, what a sorry, sorry end to all my high dreams! When a rope and the long drop through the black trap should cut short an honorable career and a useful life! And all because of a human vampire who feared his rotten lust on my soul, and drove me to murder and ruin.

But I knew my fate was written in the iron books of doom. Sooner or later I would turn on Ortali and kill him, be the consequences what they might. And I reached the end of my road. Continual torture had rendered me, I believe, partly insane. I knew that at Grimmin's Cairn, when we toiled at midnight, Ortali's life would end beneath my hands, and my own life be cast away.

Something fell out of my pocket and I picked it up. It was the piece of sharp stone I had caught up off the cairn. Looking at it moodily, I wondered what strange hands had touched it in old times, and what grim secret it helped to hide on the bare headland of Grimmin. I switched out the light and lay in the darkness, the stone still in my hand, forgotten, occupied with my own dark broodings. And I glided gradually into deep slumber.

At first I was aware that I was dreaming, as people often are. All was dim and vague, and connected in some strange way, I realized, with the bit of stone still grasped in my sleeping hand. Gigantic, chaotic scenes and landscapes and events shifted before me, like clouds that rolled and tumbled before a gale. Slowly these settled and crystallized into one distinct landscape, familiar and yet wildly strange. I saw a broad bare plain, fringed by the grey sea on one side, and a dark, rustling forest on the other; this plain was cut by a winding river, and beyond this river I saw a city--such a city as my waking eyes had never seen: bare, stark, massive, with the grim architecture of an earlier, wilder age. On the plain I saw, as in a mist, a mighty battle. Serried ranks rolled backward and forward, steel flashed like a sunlit sea, and men fell like ripe wheat beneath the blades. I saw men in wolfskins, wild and shock-headed, wielding dripping axes, and tall men in horned helmets, and glittering mail, whose eyes were cold and blue as the sea. And I saw myself.

Yes, in my dream I saw and recognized, in a semidetached way, myself. I was tall and rangily powerful; I was shockheaded and naked but for a wolf-hide girt about my loins. I ran among the ranks yelling and smiting with a red ax, and blood ran down my flanks from wounds I scarcely felt. My eyes were cold blue and my shaggy hair and beard were red.

Now for an instant I was cognizant of my dual personality, aware that I was at once the wild man who ran and smote with the gory ax, and the man who slumbered and dreamed across the centuries. But this sensation quickly faded. I was no longer aware of any personality other than that of the barbarian who ran and smote. James O'Brien had no existence; I was Red Cumal, kern of Brian Boru, and my ax was dripping with the blood of my foes.

The roar of conflict was dying away, though here and there struggling clumps of warriors still dotted the plain. Down along the river, half-naked tribesmen, waist-deep in reddening water, tore and slashed with helmeted warriors

21

whose mail could not save them from the stroke of the Dalcassian ax. Across the river a bloody, disorderly horde was staggering through the gates of Dublin.

The sun was sinking low toward the horizon. All day I had fought beside the chiefs. I had seen Jarl Sigurd fall beneath Prince Murrough's sword. I had seen Murrough himself die in the moment of victory, by the hand of a grim mailed giant whose name none knew. I had seen, in the flight of the enemy, Brodir and King Brian fall together at the door of the great king's tent.

Aye, it had been a feasting of ravens, a red flood of slaughter, and I knew that no more would the dragonprowed fleets sweep from the blue North with torch and destruction. Far and wide the Vikings lay in their glittering mail, as the ripe wheat lies after the reaping. Among them lay thousands of bodies clad in the wolf hides of the tribes, but the dead of the Northern people far outnumbered the dead of Erin. I was weary and sick of the stench of raw blood. I had glutted my soul with slaughter; now I sought plunder. And I found it-- on the corpse of a richly-clad Norse chief which lay close to the seashore. I tore off the silver-scaled corselet, the horned helmet. They fitted as if made for me, and I swaggered among the dead, calling on my wild comrades to admire my appearance, though the harness felt strange to me, for the Gaels scorned armour and fought half-naked.

In my search for loot I had wandered far out on the plain, away from the river, but still the mail-clad bodies lay thickly strewn, for the bursting of the ranks had scattered fugitives and pursuers all over the countryside, from the dark waving Wood of Tomar, to the river and the seashore. And on the seaward slope of Drumna's headland, out of sight of the city and the plain of Clontarf, I came suddenly upon a dying warrior. He was tall and massive, clad in grey mail. He lay partly in the folds of a great dark cloak, and his sword lay broken near his mighty right hand. His horned helmet had fallen from his head and his elf-locks blew in the wind that swept out of the west.

Where one eye should have been was an empty socket, arid the other eye glittered cold and grim as the North Sea, though it was glazing with approach of death. Blood oozed from a rent in his corselet. I approached him warily, a strange cold fear, that I could not understand, gripping me. Ax ready to dash out his brains, I bent over him, and recognized him as the chief who had slain Prince Murrough, and who had mown down the warriors of the Gael like a harvest.. Wherever he had fought, the Norsemen had prevailed, but in all other parts of the field, the Gaels had been irresistible.

And now he spoke to me in Norse and I understood, for had I not toiled as slave among the sea people for long bitter years?

"The Christians have overcome," he gasped in a voice whose timbre, though low-pitched, sent a curious shiver of fear through me; there was in it an undertone as of icy waves sweeping along a Northern shore, as of freezing winds whispering among the pine trees. "Doom and shadows stalk on Asgaard and hero has fallen Ragnarok. I could not be in all parts of the field at once, and now I am wounded unto death. A spear-a spear with a cross carved in the blade; no other weapon could wound me."

I realized that the chief, seeing mistily my red beard and the Norse armour I wore, supposed me to be one of his own race. But crawling horror surged darkly in the depths of my soul.

"White Christ, thou hast not yet conquered," he muttered deliriously. "Lift me up, man, and let me speak to you."

Now for some reason I complied, and, as I lifted him to a sitting posture, I shuddered and my flesh crawled at the feel of him, for his flesh was like ivory--smoother and harder than is natural for human flesh, and colder than even a dying man should be.

"I die as men die;" he muttered. "Fool, to assume the attributes of mankind, even though it was to aid the people who deify me. The gods are immortal, but flesh can perish, even when it clothes a god. Haste and bring a sprig of the magic plant-even holly-and lay it on my bosom. Aye, though it be no larger than a dagger point, it will free me from this fleshy prison I put on when I came to war with men with their own weapons. And I will shake off this flesh and stalk once more among the thundering clouds. Woe, then, to all men who bend not the knee to me! Haste; I will await your coming."

His lion-like head fell back, and feeling shudderingly under his corselet, I could distinguish no heartbeat. He was dead, as men die, but I knew that locked in that semblance of a human body, there but slumbered the spirit of a fiend of the frost and darkness.

Aye, I knew him: Odin, the Grey Man, the One-eyed, the god of the North who had taken the form of a warrior to fight for his people. Assuming the form of a human, he was subject to many of the limitations of humanity. All men knew this of the gods, who often walked the earth in the guise of men. Odin, clothed in human semblance, could he wounded by certain weapons, and even slain, but a touch of the mysterious holly, would rouse him in grisly resurrection. This task he had set me, not knowing me for an enemy; in human form he could only use human faculties, and these had been impaired by onstriding death.

My hair stood up and my flesh crawled. I tore from my body the Norse armour, and fought a wild panic that prompted me to run blind and screaming with terror across-the plain. Nauseated with fear, I gathered boulders and heaped them for a rude couch, and on it, shaking with horror, I lifted the body of the Norse god. And as the sun set and the stars came silently out, I was working with fierce energy, piling huge rocks above the corpse. Other tribesmen came up and I told them of what I was sealing up--I hoped forever. And they, shivering with horror, fell to aiding me. No sprig of magic holly should be laid on Odin's terrible bosom. Beneath these rude stones the Northern demon should slumber until the thunder of Judgment Day, forgotten by the world which had once cried out beneath his iron heel. Yet not wholly forgotten, for, as we laboured, one of my comrades said: "This shall be no longer Drumna's Headland, but the Headland of the Grey Man."

That phrase established a connection between my dream-self and my sleeping-self. I started up from sleep exclaiming: "Grey Man's Headland!"

I looked about dazedly, the furnishings of the room, faintly lighted by the starlight in the windows, seeming strange and unfamiliar until I slowly oriented myself with time and space.

"Grey Man's Headland," I repeated, "Grey Man-Greymin-Grimmin-Grimmin's Headland! Great God, the thing under the cairn!"

Shaken, I sprang up, and realized that I still gripped the piece of stone from the cairn. It is well known that inanimate objects retain psychic associations. A round stone from the plain of Jericho has been placed in the land of a hypnotized medium, and she has at once reconstructed in her mind the battle and siege of the city, and the shattering fall of the walls. I did not doubt that this bit of stone had acted as a magnet to drag my modern mind through the mists of the centuries into a life I had known before.

I was more shaken than I can describe, for the whole fantastic affair fitted in too well with certain formless vague sensations concerning the cairn which had already lingered at the back of my mind, to be dismissed as an unusually vivid dream. I felt the need of a glass of wine, and remembered that Ortali always had wine in his room. I hurriedly donned my clothes, opened my door, crossed the corridor and was about to, knock at Ortali's door, when I noticed that it was partly open, as if someone had neglected to close it carefully. I entered, switching on a light. The room was empty.

I realized what had occurred. Ortali mistrusted me; he feared to risk himself alone with me in a lonely spot at midnight. He had postponed the visit to the cairn merely to trick me, to give himself a chance to slip away alone.

My hatred for Ortali was for the moment completely submerged by a wild panic of horror at the thought of what the opening of the cairn might result in. For I did not doubt the authenticity of my dream. It was no dream; it was a fragmentary bit of memory, in which I had relived that other life of mine. Grey Man's Headland--Grimmin's

Headland, and under those rough stones that grisly corpse in its semblance of humanity. I could not hope that, imbued with the imperishable essence of an elemental spirit, that corpse had crumbled to dust in the ages.

Of my race out of the city and across those semidesolate reaches, I remember little. The night was a cloak of horror through which peered red stars like the gloating eyes of uncanny beasts, and my footfalls echoed hollowly so that repeatedly I thought some monster loped at my heels.

The straggling lights fell away behind me and I entered the region of mystery and horror. No wonder that progress had passed to the right and to the left of this spot, leaving it untouched, a blind back-eddy given over to goblin-dreams and nightmare memories. Well that so few suspected its very existence.

Dimly I saw the headland, but fear gripped me and held me aloof. I had a vague, incoherent idea of finding the ancient woman; Meve MacDonnal. She was grown old in the mysteries and traditions of the mysterious land. She could aid me, if indeed the blind fool Ortali loosed on the world the forgotten demon men once worshipped in the North.

A figure loomed suddenly in the starlight and I caromed against him, almost upsetting him. A stammering voice in a thick brogue protested with the petulance of intoxication. It was a burly longshoreman returning to his: cottage, no doubt, from some late revel in a tavern. I seized him and shook him, my eyes glaring wildly in the starlight.

"I am looking for Meve MacDonnal! Do you know her? Tell me, you fool! Do you know old Meve MacDonnal?"

It was as if my words sobered him as suddenly as a dash of icy water in his face. In the starlight I saw his face glimmer whitely and a catch of fear was at his throat. He sought to cross himself with an uncertain hand.

"Meve MacDonnal! Are ye mad? What would ye be doin' with her?"

"Tell me!" I shrieked, shaking him savagely. "Where is Meve MacDonnal--"

"There!" he gasped, pointing with a shaking hand, where dimly in the night something loomed against the shadows. "In the name of the holy saints, begone, by ye madman or devil, and rave an honest man alone! There, there ye'll find Meve MacDonnal--where they laid her, full three hundred years ago!"

Half heeding his words, I flung him aside with a fierce exclamation, and, as I raced across the weed-grown plain, I heard the sound of his lumbering flight. Half blind with panic, I came to the low structure the man had pointed out. And floundering deep in weeds, my feet sinking into the musty mould, I realized with a shock that I was in the ancient graveyard on the inland side of Grimmin's Headland, into which I had seen Meve MacDonnal disappear the evening before. I was close by the door of the largest tomb, and with an eerie premonition I leaned close, seeking to make out the deeply carven inscription. And partly by the dim light of the stars and partly by the touch of my tracing fingers, I made out the words and figures, in the half-forgotten Gaelic of three centuries ago: Meve MacDonnal-1556-1640.

With a cry of horror, I recoiled and, snatching out the crucifix she had given me, made to hurl it into the darkness--but it was as if an invisible hand caught my wrist. Madness and insanity--but I could not doubt: Meve MacDonnal had come to me from the tomb wherein she had rested for three hundred years to give me, the ancient, ancient relic entrusted to her so long ago by her priestly kin. The memory of her words came to me, and the memory of Ortali and the Grey Man. From a lesser horror I turned squarely to a greater, and ran swiftly toward the headland which loomed dimly against the stars toward the sea.

As I crossed the ridge I saw, in the starlight, the cairn, and the figure that toiled gnome-like above it. Ortali, with his accustomed, almost superhuman energy, had dislodged many of the boulders; and as I approached, shaking with horrified anticipation, I saw him tear aside the last layer, and I heard his savage cry of triumph that froze me in my trace some yards behind him, looking down from the slope. An unholy radiance rose from the cairn, and I saw, in the north, the aurora came up suddenly with terrible beauty, paling the starlight. All about the cairn pulsed a weird light, turning the rough stones to a cold shimmering silver, and in this glow I saw Ortali, all heedless, cast aside his pick and lean gloatingly over the aperture he had made-and I saw there the helmeted head, reposing on the couch of stones where I, Red Cumal, had placed it so long ago. I saw the inhuman terror and beauty of that awesome carven face, in which was neither human weakness, pity nor mercy. I saw the soul-freezing glitter of the one eye, which stared wide open in a fearful semblance of life. All up and down the tall mailed figure shimmered and sparkled cold darts arid gleams of icy light; like the northern lights that blazed in the shuddering skies. Aye, the Grey Man lay as I had left him more than nine hundred years before, without trace of rust or rot or decay.

And now as Ortali leaned forward to examine his find, a gasping cry broke from his lips--for the sprig of holly, worn in his lapel in defiance of "Nordic superstition," slipped from its place, and in the weird glow I plainly saw it fall upon the mighty mailed breast of the figure, where it blazed suddenly with a brightness too dazzling for human eyes. My cry was echoed by Ortali. The figure moved; the mighty limbs flexed, tumbling the shining stones aside. A new gleam lighted the terrible eye, and a tide of life flooded and animated the carven features.

Out of the cairn he rose, and the northern lights played terribly about him. And the Grey Man changed ad altered in horrific transmutation. The human features faded like a fading mask; the armour fell from his body and crumbled to dust as it fell; and the fiendish spirit of ice and frost and darkness that the sons of the North deified as Odin, stood nakedly and terribly, in the stars. About his grisly head played lightnings and the shuddering gleams of the aurora. His towering anthropomorphic form was dark as shadow and gleaming as ice; his horrible crest reared colossally against the vaulting arch of the sky.

Ortali cowered, screaming wordlessly, as the taloned, malformed hands reached for him. In the shadowy, indescribable features of the Thing, there was no tinge of gratitude toward the man who had released it--only a demoniac gloating and a demoniac hate for all the sons of men. I saw the shadowy arms shoot out and strike. I heard Ortali scream once--a single, unbearable screech that broke short at the shrillest pitch. A single instant a blinding blue glare burst about him, lighting his convulsed features and his upward-rolling eyes; then his body was dashed earthward as by an electric shock, so savagely that I distinctly heard the splintering of his bones. But Ortali was dead before he touched the ground--dead, shriveled and blackened, exactly like a man blasted by a thunderbolt, to which cause, indeed, men later ascribed his death.

The slavering monster that had slain him lumbered now toward me, shadowy, tentacle-like arms outspread, the pale starlight making a luminous pool of his great inhuman eye, his frightful talons dripping with I know not what elemental forces to blast the bodies and souls of men.

But I flinched not, and in that instant I feared him not, neither the horror of his countenance nor the threat of his thunderbolt dooms. For in a blinding white flame had come to me the realization of why Meve MacDonnal had come from her tomb to bring me the ancient cross which had lain in her bosom for three hundred years, gathering unto itself unseen forces of good and light, which war forever against the shapes of lunacy and shadow.

As I plucked from my garments the ancient cross, I felt the play of gigantic unseen forces in the air about me. I was but a pawn in the game--merely the hand that held the relic of holiness, that was the symbol of the powers opposed forever against the fiends of darkness. As I held it high, from it shot a single shaft of white light, unbearably pure, unbearably white, as if all the awesome forces of Light were combined in the symbol and loosed in one concentrated arrow of wrath against the monster of darkness. And with a hideous shriek the demon reeled back, shriveling before my eyes. Then, with a great rush of vulture-like wings, he soared into the stars, dwindling dwindling among the play of the flaming fires and the lights of the haunted skies, fleeing back into the dark limbo which gave him birth, God only knows how many grisly eons ago.

www.ingramcontent.com/pod-product-compliance
Lightning Source LLC
Chambersburg PA
CBHW030242180626
46810CB00008B/3251